For the students of SHES, who never miss an opportunity to giggle.
May your lives be filled with smiles, laughter, and joy.
--M.A.

For Venesia Ann Blythe, a woman who knew how to laugh
and always brought smiles to our faces.
--Z.M.

Illustrations by Zoe Mellors

Editing by Lor Bingham and Chelsea Tornetto

Book Design by Zoe Mellors

Paperback ISBN: 978-1-7357836-2-8
Hardcover ISBN: 978-1-7357836-3-5

LCCN:2020924806

Visit www.meaghanaxel.com

Psssst...
What are you guys doing in here? I think these readers want a turn with this book.

We're trying to get a closer look at this book because the grown-ups want to know its purpose.

Well, what's the problem?

We've never read a book quite like this before--it is **impossible** to describe.

I'm **NOT** Like Other Books

Written By Meaghan Axel ★ Illustrated By Zoe Mellors

I'll help you. Let's invite these readers to join us too.

I mean, it's a kid's book!

How hard can it be for all of us to figure out its purpose?

Oh, hello there! Since you've opened me,
I should probably warn you--

I'm not like other books.

I'm different, and probably not what you're expecting.
So, if you're hoping I'll entertain you or teach you something new,
you should probably put me down and find another book.

The readers are
still here.
Oh dear.
Well, what kind of
book are you?
What's your
purpose?
The grown-ups
need to know.

Ever since I was written, I've never really fit in.

All the other picture books on my shelf seem a bit juvenile.

The nonfiction books are always trying to teach me something like,

"Flamingos eat with their heads upside down."

What am I supposed to do with that information?

Don't worry. You won't learn anything new by reading me.

Hey, do you know why *flamingos* stand with one leg up?

Because they would fall if they lifted up *BOTH* legs!

Don't even get me started on chapter books!

They are **full** of cliffhangers.

I would never leave you hanging.

Which reminds me of the time I was minding my own business and then I heard someone whisper, *"It's him, I've finally found him after all these years,"* and two large hands reached for my spine.

I'm the kind of book that doesn't rhyme.
Who has time to make all their lines rhyme?
Believe me, I don't.
Rhyme my words?
No, I won't.

What rhymes with orange?

Um, no.
It doesn't.

I avoid tricking readers into making funny noises like,

"Boomshakalakawoohoo!"
or
"Kerplunkerdorfffff!"

You don't have to worry about feeling silly or spitting all over my pages when you read me out loud.

I don't ask for favors.

I would never request that you hold
my page down right here and sweep out all these dust
bunnies and cobwebs.

You're doing me a favor already by reading me.

I'm not the kind of book that uses toilet humor just to get a few laughs.

You won't find any jokes about *passing gas* in here.

I'm not the kind of book with adventure.
My characters aren't superheroes who go on epic escapades
and teach bad guys a lesson.
There isn't even a dinosaur in here, not one!

I don't show you cool yoga poses or encourage you to
practice mindfulness. I won't even inspire you to be a
better person. I don't have any words of wisdom like,
"Make it a great day, or not-the choice is yours!"

And, you certainly won't find any monsters, ghosts, vampires, or zombies in here.

Spooky ghouls give me the creeps.

Trust me, I'm not trying to scare you.

I can assure you, I'm not even going to warn you about pushing that *big, shiny button* over there.

Go ahead and push it if you want to.

You probably won't like what happens though.

I'm not going to try to teach you a lesson like,
"You probably shouldn't push buttons if you don't know what they do."

You're a smart reader. You know right from wrong.
You understand that the right thing to do now is to spin me around a few times so the rest of this book isn't upside down.

The lesson is, we probably should have chosen a different book!

The grown-ups are going to want a lesson...

I'm not the kind of book that teaches
you about the alphabet.

You probably already know that the
26 letters in the alphabet make 40 distinct sounds.

I wasn't written to enrich your vocabulary.

**It is improbable that perusing my pages will
ameliorate your lexicon.**

You won't find my pages filled with unicorns, glitter, princesses, or fairies.

That's a shame because sloths are *so trendy* right now.

Actually, I think everyone moved on to narwhals while waiting for sloths to happen.

So, do you really want to know what kind of book I am?
The grown-ups need to know my purpose?
Are you sure they can handle the truth?
Okay, I'll tell you, but I don't think my answer will make
the grown-ups happy.

I am the kind of book that is a

COMPLETE WASTE OF TIME!

Have a few minutes to spare, but don't want to start
reading something too captivating?

I'm your book!

I promise you, I will waste your time like it's my job.

No other book can say that as confidently as I can.

And for that, I am truly an original.

We're NOT like any other team!

Meet the Author

Meaghan Axel is a grown-up who has probably asked many children to find the purpose of countless stories during her career as an English teacher. However, her favorite moments in the classroom have always been the ones filled with shared, spontaneous laughter and amusement. Meaghan is now an elementary school librarian on the Eastern Shore of Maryland. She is probably chuckling over a silly story right now. Meaghan loves yoga, nature, meditation, and humor--especially when it is shared with her husband and daughter. Look for Axel's Powerful Me children's book series, which inspires children to make mindful choices to improve their self-esteem and relationships. Meaghan hopes her books will help children giggle, grow, and bond with others.

Visit www.meaghanaxel.com for free learning activities and resources.

Meet the illustrator

Zoe Mellors is an illustrator based in the UK who loves reading and drawing. From getting her hands messy when she was finger painting, to doodling in the margins of her school books, Zoe has always been inspired to create beauty. She studied illustration at the University of Lincoln, where she fell in love with the idea of telling a story through art. Zoe is passionate about using her art to tell tales that will make readers fall in love with books just as she did as a child.

To see more of Zoe's drawings, please visit: www.zoemellorsillustration.com

Made in the USA
Middletown, DE
15 December 2022

18681635R00018